Karen's Wild Adventures

Katharine L Niffen

Published by Katharine L Niffen, 2021.

This is a work of fiction. Similarities to real people, places, or events are entirely coincidental.

KAREN'S WILD ADVENTURES

First edition. August 5, 2021.

ISBN: 979-8201024185

Written by Katharine L Niffen.

This book is a work of fiction, names, characters, business, events, and incidents are the product of the Author's imagination, and any resemblance to actual persons living or dead or actual events is purely confidential.

I dedicate this book to my son and his family. For always believing in me and supporting my writing. I am dedicating it also to my parents. Who will remain in my heart always!

In addition, I dedicate it to my best friends and their families. Who became a part of my family. I greatly appreciate your patience as I bugged you through the process. As well as supporting me in my dreams.

I love each and every one of you. I would like to thank each and every one of you. My life would not be the same without all of you. Thank you so much for everything you do.

The book tells the story of a woman named Karen. She is an archaeologist who studies ancient artifacts. As Karen travels on her journeys, she encounters strange and mysterious creatures.

Inquire about ancient artifacts. Never seen by anyone in the world before. The discovery of diamonds, gold, and rare rubies. On Karen's first journey. Exploring ancient ruins that were both dangerous and exciting. Unfortunately, Karen's eight companions were all killed. When she went to the Unexplained island.

Her life was on the line several times. She encountered magical things along the way. There were also creatures that she believed were from another realm. It was a journey unlike any other she had ever experienced. Until she went on a cruise ship and ended up on the Black Rose, the pirate ship. As she went through a time portal. Her battles involve pirates and strange sea creatures from a time long ago. In both of her adventures, she gained a great deal of wealth.

They were two adventures she would never forget in her life. The kind of adventures she never wanted to go on again. The kind that made her brave in the sight of danger.

Unexplained Island

Karen is twenty-four years old. A single woman with long blond hair. Beautiful blue eyes and a body of an athlete. Additionally, she enjoys traveling the world as an archaeologist. Her specialty is ancient artifacts. Who lives in a small Illinois town. She has dreamed of going on an adventure for a long time. It would be a journey she would never forget. The journey will take place in a distant land. Almost no one knows what lies in this unknown land.

Having planned to leave on the weekend, Karen was eager to leave. She packed her bag with everything she thought she would need. She packed the essentials for her journey by taking a compass, rope, machete, sleeping bag, and tent alone. Her pack also contained some food.

Waking up at seven a.m. on Saturday. She was eager to leave. She hurried up to eat breakfast. As well as getting dressed. Then she grabbed her bag and headed out the door. After getting in her car, she drove to the airport. To take a plane to the coast of Africa.

Upon arriving on the African coast, she had to find a ship to take her to a mysterious Island. It was referred to as the Unexplained island. There were several stories told by the locals about this land. Some say it was inhabited by monsters never before seen. Others claim the land was said to be enchanted by magic. There was something that scared the locals. So bad that they all stayed away.

Karen spent five days trying to find a shipowner who would take her to the island. Her main challenge will be finding a group of brave people willing to join her on this journey. There are not many men and women brave enough to attempt this adventure. She was able to find five men and three women. With her offer of an adventure of a lifetime, Karen was able to entice them all.

After loading the ship, the group set sail for the mysterious island. The journey took ten days. It was early morning when they got close enough to the Island. When they all got there, they had to get into roll boats to get to the island. Landing on a short sandy beach. As soon as they unloaded their boats, they set out into the jungle. Karen's excitement in exploring the island was contagious.

They were excited to see if they would find any rare valuables. Karen was wondering if any of the locals' stories were real. As they walked through the jungle they noticed that it started to get thicker. So they were forced to use their machetes. The day was spent hiking through the jungle. As night fell, they cleared an area and started setting up camp. So they could spend the night.

During the night, they each took turns to sleep. Therefore, they could have someone on watch, as none of them knew the dangers of the island. Karen decided it would be best to sleep for four hours before changing the guard at night watch.

There were no problems during the night, and everyone had a good sleep. They all got up early to head out. They still need their machetes to walk through the jungle. In the afternoon, they came across some ancient ruins. Which Karen found very exciting. As Karen approached the ruins, she found ancient writings on the wall. There were some people in Karen's group who were scared by this. They feared some of the stories the locals told were true.

Karen didn't care about the stories she heard; she wanted to check out the ancient ruins. A place that no one else has ever seen in thousands of years. They just had to figure out what the ancient writings said. To find their way into the ruins. Karen and her group were able to figure out the meaning of the writings in the early night. Consequently, Karen decided to explore the ruins the following day.

It was too exciting for Karen and her group to sleep that night. They were talking about what they were hoping to find inside the ruins. Some wished for gold, while others hoped for rubies and diamonds. Karen was imaging finding some rare artifacts. Karen knew if they found any of these things they would be known all around the world for finding such rare items.

As morning approached everyone prepared to enter the ruins. They got some touchers ready and lit. They had to move symbols around on the wall to open the secret door in order to enter the ruins. As soon as the door opened, the fire lit up the hallway. Then Karen saw more ancient writing on the walls of the hallway.

In some of the writings, there was a warning of danger if they continued. Another type of writing described creatures that guarded the ruins. At the end of the hallway, where it split into two directions. A different warning said, "he who chooses the wrong path will surely die in excruciating pain".

Karen decided that they should follow the path that led to the right. There was something creepy about the hallway as it grew darker. It was only possible to see twenty feet ahead of them. Suddenly, the group started hearing strange noises. Several of the noises sounded like squeaks and cracks in the walls and flooring. Some other noises sound like animals lurking in the ruins.

Upon hearing the sounds the group started getting goosebumps. The sounds some heard terrified them. Some of them were afraid to explore any further in the ruins. Karen, however, encouraged them to go further into the ruins. As they turned a corner in the damp, dark hallway. One of the group members named Steve stepped on a brick and noticed it move under his foot. A blast of metal spikes ripped through the wall. Nearly missed hitting any member of the group.

Within seconds of the metal spikes ripping through the walls, the floor opened into a deep pit filled with darts. For Karen and her group to jump over the pit, they had to use a rope. Having gotten over the pit, Karen advised her group to proceed carefully. Suddenly there was the sound of an animal in front of them. Some wanted to turn back for fear, they took the path of painful death, the old writing mentions. Karen encouraged the group to move forward. As they moved forward, they were careful to move slowly.

The hallway suddenly opened into a huge room. Huge pillars surrounded the doorway on both sides. From touches, a fire lit up the room by themselves. Pillars lined the walls of the room. There was a huge chair in front of the room. Karen and her group thought it looked like a throne. Statues of creatures unknown to man adorned both sides of the chair.

The statues had large teeth and longhorns on their heads. They had a single big eye in the middle of their head. Their backs are adorned with big wings, and they stood on four legs. A red cushion covered a chair between the statues that were covered in cobwebs. On the chair was carved in ancient writings that said " the queen of all beast ".

The gray damp walls were inscribed with a legend of a queen who would wear the crown of the beast. One who wears the crown rules them all. Karen advised everyone to keep their eyes peeled for the crown. After searching the room, no further items were found. So they searched for another door to continue exploring. As if by magic, the statues began to move.

The statues growled as they moved. Karen and her group were horrified by what they saw and heard.

The statues came after Karen and her group. They were fighting for their lives. To fight the statues, the group pulled out their machetes. They attacked them from all sides with everything they had. The statues swung at Karen and her group. Karen and her group struck back hitting the statues with their machetes. In the fight, four members fought against each statue. They fought until they knocked the heads off. It took about an hour from the beginning of the fight to the end. After finally demolishing the statues. A door appeared behind the chair.

When Karen and her group interred the door. They found three hallways. There is one going left, one going right, and one going straight. To explore the ruins better, Karen divided her group into three. Three people to each group. Each group taking a hallway. Karen's group, which includes Mike, and Lura explored the hallway straight ahead.

Another group including Steve, Mary, and Andy went down the hallway to the left. The last group includes John, Tim, and Terry who went down the hallway on the right. Karen saw more writing on the walls. The inscription said, "beware of the beast within". As they walked further down the hallway. In a flash, the walls started closing in. Karen and her group started to run for their lives. It took them only a few minutes to escape the hallway before the walls closed.

After escaping the hallway, the group entered another room. The room seemed to look like more of a dining room. It had one long table in the middle of the room with two long benches on each side. At the end were two chairs. Everything was covered in cobwebs. On the other side of the room was a huge door along with two other doors one on each side of the room.

On the table were five chests. A sign said, "Choose wisely, you only have one choice, if you chose more, then you would die". Gold and diamonds covered every chest. Karen and her group talked about which chest they should pick. One chest alone would give Karen and her group a lot of money. A decision was made to open the middle chest.

After opening the chest, they discovered gold coins and rubies. Karen and her group were so excited about what they found. They divided the gold and rubes and packed them in their bags. Karen kept the chest for herself. After loading up their treasure they decided to go through the door on the right.

However, one of Karen's group members returned after the other left through the door. Lura turned back and decided to take another chest. Upon grabbing the chest, the spikes came streaming down from the roof. Going through the head and shoulders of the Lura and all the way to the floor. Instantly killing her on the spot. When Karen and Mike heard Lura scream they turned back to see what happened. When entering the room they found Lura dead.

Karen and Mike bolted from the room. Afraid that something will happen to them as well. They ran out the door and down the hallway.

After doing this, they heard growing behind them. They ran faster in an attempt to escape whatever was behind them. After running for quite some time, they could hear thumping noises behind them getting closer.

They were afraid to look back to see what was chasing them. They prayed that they could escape what was behind them. Karen started seeing doors closer and closer as she ran. Hoping they can find one to open an escape.

They checked each door until they found one that would open. As they open the door and shut it behind them just in time. Suddenly, they heard banging on the door and screams from inside the room. Looking around, they couldn't find anyone. They weren't able to explain where the scream came from.

There was only a bed in the room. With curtains tied to all four posts of the bed. As well as draped in cobwebs. The two screeched throughout the room to see if they could find anything. There was a persistent banging on the door. They tried to figure out a way out for their own safety.

The thing that was banging on the door stopped. Karen and Mike were still frightened to open the door. As they were still frightened by the sounds of screaming in the room. Being unable to see anyone in the room, they chose to stay in the room. Karen prayed that the other two groups were all safe.

In addition, she wonders if the screaming they heard was from one of the other two groups. As screams seemed to echo inside the ruins. Although Karen loved going on adventures, she did not want to fight for her life while she was doing so. Several hours had passed without any banging on the door. So Karen and Mike decided to leave the room. In order to make sure there was no obstruction in the hallway, Karen slowly opened the door. They headed down the hallway until they came to a split. The hallway split into two directions. They decided to take the one going left.

As they walked down the hallway they ran into Steve and Mary. Andy died in that group, so two remained just as in Karen's group. Each group shared what had happened to the one missing member. The screams Karen and Mike heard were from the missing person in the other group.

The two groups decided to join up together to be safer. For they have been in the ruins for two days now. One whole day has passed since they last saw the third group. Each of them prayed and hoped they were all safe. The place in the hallway where the two groups meet. This hallway led to dark and narrow paths. Spiraling stairs marked the end of the path.

The group heard more screaming as they climbed up the stairs. Knowing the dangers that were behind them, they decided on going forward. As they reached the top of the stairs. They interred a room at the end of which were two chairs. Sitting beside each other with two statues beside them. They looked like the first two statues they saw when they entered the ruins.

Rolls of benches lined the sides of the room. At the end of the benches were smaller statues. That looked like the bigger one. Unlike any other room they had seen so far, this room wasn't covered in cobwebs. In the two big chairs at the end of the room. Where crowns sit in the middle of the chairs. Beside one chair was a sword leaning up against it.

There were the words ruler of the holy ones above the chairs in ancient writing. In front of the chairs were two chests covered in gold. There are ancient writings on them, and one of the writings says only the chosen may open. According to the other, only the holy are capable of opening the chests.

After searching the room for traps, Karen and her group went to the chests to see what was inside. The group talked for a few moments before letting Steve open the chest. Steve vanished into thin air when he touched one of the chests. So the group decided to search the room again. This time Karen found a secret box under one of the chairs. She accidentally pushed down on one of the chair's arms on the right side of the room.

Upon opening the box, she discovered ancient scrolls. Opening the scrolls one read in ancient writings. Only the one with a pure heart can open the chests. Another one reads only the one that can see evil in another can open the chests. Those who opened the chests would bring destruction to the world. Those were the words on the scrolls. The last scroll was both a warring and a blessing at the same time. It read that whoever wears the crown will be the richest in the whole world. He who wears the crown, however, will release all creatures upon the earth and suffer a horrific death.

After talking to the group they decided to leave the chests and the crown's right where they were. Afraid of what will happen. Karen also put back the scrolls to leave the room as they found it. As she put the scrolls back she noticed a door in the corner of the room.

They all left the room and prayed that the other group would leave everything the same if they came into the room too. As they left the room down a hall so narrow that they had to walk sideways to go through it. They walked along this path for approximately thirty feet before they reached the outside of the ruins.

When they got outside, John, who was in the third group, was there. Terry and Tim died in the ruin. They all shared what happened to the missing people in the groups. Nine people went into the ruins and only four people came out. Karen told the other that Lura died from spikes going through her body when she went back to get another chest. Andy was killed by a stature that attacked him and his group. The group heard from John that Terry and Tim died at the hands of a mysterious creature. John was informed by Karen that Steve vanished into thin air when he touched a chest. Karen and the others talked about what they wanted to do next. Karen explained that she wanted to explore the rest of the island. Some of the others wanted to go back home. After talking for the rest of the day the groups decided to spit up. Mary and Mike agreed to keep going with Karen to explore the Island. John decided to go home; they had enough of the Island.

They all decided to part ways in the morning. When they all got up they said their goodbyes. Sending each other good wishes. As Karen and her group headed deeper into the jungle. To explore the mysteries of the Island, praying for their safety. Two more days of walking into the jungle brought them to a ruin that appeared to be a temple. At the bottom of the ruin, it had stairs going up it on all sides. Halfway up there were two doors with stairs in the middle of them.

Karen and the group decided to go up the stairs first to see what's at the top of the ruin. After checking out the top of the ruin then they will come back down to check out what's inside the ruin. As they reached the top, they saw a slab of stone that looked like a table with stone bowls. Their sizes appeared different, and the inside of the bowls appeared to be red. That's all that was at the top of the ruin. Which made Karen and her group believe more that it was some kind of a temple.

After checking out the top they all decided to go back down the stairs to the doors. When they reached the doors they entered the one on the left side. Going into the door they entered a wet dark hallway. They let the touchers so they could see. They walked all the way down the hallway into a large room.

In this room, they saw one more door that was to the right of them. Also in the room, they saw an item that looked like a bed, two chairs, and a table. At the end of the bed, there was a large chest. On the walls were the same ancient writings that were in the other ruins. According to the writings, the blood of the innocent will bring peace. Each organ brings a different wealth. Each body part must be burnt to feed the gods.

Next, they read a warning that said behold the false sacrifice. Which freaked them all out a little. After they read the writings on the wall they hear noises that sounded like people crying. As they looked around the room they didn't see anyone. So they decided to look into the chest to see if there were any treasures inside.

Once they opened the chest they found silver and a few pieces of gold. They spit the gold between them along with the sliver. After they packed all the gold and silver into their bags. They headed towards the door they did not come in. As they got in front of the door they heard a voice. "If you take what is not yours, we will come after you."

Karen and the group decided to take the treasure they found with them. To risk the chance to show the world what they have found. After entering the door, they heard a deep creepy voice saying, "You will die for taking what is not yours". As they walked through the door and down the narrow hallway. Which took them outside.

Once they got outside the two doors vanished before them. When they got to the ground they heard a blast. That made them look around and when they looked up they saw a blast of fire coming from the top of the temple. A voice said, "You will be sacrificed to the gods as a result of your crimes". Karen and her group ran from the temple as fast as they could. They ran deeper into the jungle. When they ran, they could hear something chasing them.

As they ran upon a wooden bridge. As they were crossing the wooden bridge over a deep river, that was several feet under the bridge. They could feel it begin to break. As they reached the middle of the bridge one of Karen's feet broke through the bridge. While she was getting help to be pulled up on the bridge. All of a sudden the ropes on the bridge broke. Causing Karen and her group to fall on the bridge and hold on for their lives.

As they fell on the bridge the last of the ropes that held the bridge together broke. Hurling Karen and her group into the side of a cliff. Therefore, they had to climb up the piece of the bridge that they were holding onto. So they could reach safety. They heard screams of disappointment as they reached the top.

Karen thought they were safe from what was chasing them before. As they rested at the top to catch their breath. They decided to eat the last bit of food and drink the last bit of water they had. As soon as they finished eating, they headed back to the jungle. They walked for the rest of the day before setting up camp for the night.

Taking turns sleeping at night so they could be safe. Halfway into the night, creepy strange noises echoed throughout the island. Keeping Karen and her group up for being scared of what was out there. Now believing what the locals said about the island was true. As they wondered if they made a mistake coming to the Island. But Karen was determined to keep exploring the Island no matter what.

As the sun was coming up the group packed up all their stuff to get ready to head out. As they hoped they would find food and water to last them through the rest of their trip. They walked for a day when they found water and some food to hold them over for about four days. The water came from an underground source. Which meant it was safe to drink. The food they ate was some berries and a rabbit. They also got some twigs and plants that were edible.

That was where they decided to camp for the night. The crazy noises echoed throughout the night just like the night before. Throughout the night, Karen and her group forced themselves to sleep a little bit. As morning approached they ate a handful of berries before starting their walk through more of the jungle.

They walked for a half a day when they reached a field in the middle of the jungle. There was tall grass taller than Karen's group. They still needed a machete to get through it. A couple of hours into the tall grass. They came across what looked like a circle made out of the grass. It was all pushed down in a way no human could do.

This confused Karen and her group. They still could not explain all the weird things that were happening on this Island. Was it inhabited by creatures or with some kind of magical being? Karen and her group examined the grass circle they found. They spent the rest of the day examining the circle. They even spent the night at the grass circle hoping to find something that would explain what they found.

In the middle of the night, they heard something moving around in the tall grass. As it got later in the night whatever was moving in the grass got closer. As Karen and her group set by the fire which they were hoping would keep whatever was moving around in the dark grass away from them.

They soon came to realize the fire was not going to keep them safe. Six creatures emerged from the tall grass. Started to attack Karen and her group. As Karen and others raised their machetes against the creatures, they were able to defend themselves. The creatures were black in color. The creatures had three red glowing eyes and two long horns on their heads. They have razor-sharp teeth, as well as long fangs. They stood on four legs and were taller than a Kodiak bear. The rest of the night was spent fighting off the creatures.

The group only ended up with a few small wounds. As they bandaged each other up they talked about the creatures that attacked them. Trying to figure out what kind of animal that attacked. After getting bandaged up they checked out the area to see if they could find any evidence of the creatures that attacked them.

All they found was some fur that was covered in a green substance that looked like blood. This just confused the group more. They knew no animal would have green blood. As they talked to one another they knew something strange was on the Island. But was it magical or was it from another time? Before man even existed in this world.

It was a question the group determined to find out. It was now decided that they would continue to go forward into the midst of the jungle. In order to unravel the mysteries of the island. So the group traveled through the tall grass until they reached the other side and reached the edge of the jungle again.

Where they saw what looked like small ruin buildings. There were six of them in a circle. In the middle of the building was an altar. As Karen and her group entered the area of the buildings. They decided to examine each one to check if there were any things that would help them understand. The events that were going on in the Island.

They were going to check out each building. In the first building, they went into all they saw were what looked like beds all around the room. They were even stacked upon each other. Karen counted the beds and it seemed to have thirteen of them in the room. Since there was nothing else in the room they moved to the next building. In it, they saw the exact same thing that was in the first building. Nothing but what looked like thirteen beds.

So they entered the third building where they saw a big round table with an opening on one end. It seemed to be big enough to hold enough people that filled up all the beds. The table and benches that surrounded the outer side of the table and the inner side of the table were the only things in the room. It seemed to be the weirdest bunch of buildings that any of them have seen.

When they entered the fourth building they saw one big chair straight across from the door and back against the wall. The floor was made of dirt like the other buildings. The chair was the only thing in the room. The building was creeping the group out more than before.

When they entered the fifth building they saw what looked like a place they stored food or something. It had what looked like shelves with bowls of all different sizes and shapes. The bowls were made out of stone.

So now they entered the last building what they saw was a statue. It looked similar to the ones they saw in the first ruin they explored. It just confused Karen and the group. Was this statue the thing worshiped by anyone who lived here or by any entity that lived here? Stone bowls surrounded the bottom of the statue. This was the only thing in the building.

They decided to move to the object in the center of the buildings that looked something like an altar. What they found were some ancient writings. In the writing, it says, "For the gods, a sacrifice must be made".

At the bottom of the stone, the altar was a stone bowl. The inside of the bowl was red.

The group was wounding what was going on in the strange island. Karen and her group wondered what would be next for them. Karen was determined that they would discover what is making this island so dangerous. They decided to camp out for the night at the building site.

Where they thought they would be safe from whatever lurked outside the building waiting to harm them. During the night strange noises echoed throughout the building. But Karen and the rest of her group had to force themselves to get some rest that night.

When morning arrived they headed into the jungle. This part of the jungle was dark and aerie it sent chills up their spine. As Karen realized why the locals were so scared of the island and why they wanted to stay away from it. The more Karen and her group went into the jungle the stranger it got.

They didn't make it far when they came across another strange ruin. This one looked like half of it was built into a large tree. With what looked like a door in the tree. The group wanted to check out this strange ruin and to see how it was built in a tree. As they walked into the door it opened up wide inside.

When they got inside they could not believe their eyes. How could it get so big on the inside when it was so small on the outside. This ruin didn't meet any kind of logic. This shouldn't have been possible in any way. It had to be some kind of magic that made this ruin. It made Karen and her group excited to explore the inside of this ruin.

So they went deeper into the ruin. Hoping to find some answer to the strange land. As they got deeper they saw some strange ancient writing that seemed to glow in the dark. The writing didn't match the ones in the other ruins. Karen tried to understand the writings but it was nothing she had seen before.

Karen could not understand them at all. So Karen and the others just keep going. When they noticed the writings seem to follow them as they walked down the hallway. They looked down in front of them and saw glowing eyes watching them. But Karen and the others believed it was some kind of thick and it was not going to stop them.

As they keep walking straight the eyes seem to move backward like they were trying to stay away from Karen and her group. Then suddenly a door appeared in front of Karen and the others. They had no option but to enter through the door. Their eyes were drawn to two creatures that looked like the statues they had seen all over the island so far.

They seemed to be frozen in place. They seemed to be floating in the air. But the creature's eyes seem to follow Karen and the others as they move into the room and into another hallway. Karen and her team were expecting to be attacked at any moment. So they were being careful with every step they took.

While this ruin was entirely different from other ruins, there must have been something that tied them all together somehow. Was it magic or something out of this world that made these ruins? That has been here for around a thousand years. There had to be a way to find out what all the answers were.

As Karen and the others came to the end of the hallway. They entered a room that kind of looked like the rooms in the other ruins. In this room, it had one big chair and one smaller chair setting at the end of the room. On each side of the chairs was a chest. Covered in gold and diamonds.

The walls of the room were also lined with pillars. A red rug was laid out in front of the two chairs coming from the door. On each side of the rugs was a roll of small statutes that looked like the other statutes seen all over the island. They were all facing the two chairs. The gold chairs were topped with red cushions and a purple fabric flowed from behind them. Making it appear that real royalty lived in the ruins.

They were also ancient writings on the walls that look like the writings in all the other ruins. These walls were carved with the phrase

"Upon the throne set the gods of all life bow down and serve for all life depends upon it." Written in ancient text.

Karen and the others search the room from top to bottom before seeing what was in the chests. All they found was a door to the left of the room in the middle of two pillars.

After the search was done they went to the chest beside the small chair. The only way to open the chest was to figure out the code. Which were three ancient symbols out of twelve. The three symbols had to line up in the perfect order. After trying multiple times Karen and her team found the right symbols. Which were a crown, a creature, and a throne. As soon as they lined up the symbol the chest popped open.

Which was filled with gold and diamonds. Which they all split between them. They placed their gold and diamonds into their bags before moving on to the next chest. To open this chest they needed a special key that was in the shape of a crown. Ancient writings on the chest said, "To him who holds the crown the treasure belongs".

They all search the room again for the key to the chest. Karen found the key in the mix of her part of the treasure that they got out of the other chest. After finding the key they all followed Karen to the other chest. To see what was inside it. When Karen opened the chest they all saw a small dagger that was made out of gold. On the end of the handle was a rare Rubie and laced with diamonds all around the handle of the dagger.

Everyone agreed that Karen should keep the dagger for herself since she was the reason they were all there in the first place. Leaving both empty chests, because they were too heavy to carry. All of them left the room through the door between two pillars. Going into yet another narrow hallway. A thin veil of light emanates from the touches in the hallway. Lighting up the ancient writings on the walls.

They were a mixture of the writing that Karen could read and the strange writing that no one could read. So Karen could only read half of the writings which didn't make sense to anyone when she read them.

They didn't know if they should worry about danger. Are expected to find riches like never before.

So all they could do was walk further down the hallway until they came to two rooms. Now they had to decide which door they would go into first. After talking for a while they chose to explore the room on the right first. The only thing that lit up the room was the touches that they were caring. It only lit up around two feet of an area around them.

Which made it a little harder for them to explore the room. Karen and the others were slower in checking out the room. As they checked out the room, they saw two slabs made from stone that looked like tables. One on each side of the room. On the slabs, there was gold fabric running down the middle of them. And in the middle of the fabric was a candle holder that held three candles.

On each side of the candleholders was a chest made out of silver. At the end of each table, there was a gold chair with purple cushions. Placed on the table in front of each chair was a crown. It had five rubies placed on each crown.

Each person decided they should open up a chest. To open each chest, Karen had to use her dagger. That she got out of the other chest. Two of the chests contained gold. Which they split between them all. One of the other ones contained diamonds and rubies. In the last chest, there was a scroll written in the ancient text saying " For he who holds the golden dagger will destroy them all".

At that moment the others looked at Karen with fear in their eyes. Because they knew that a majority of the warnings they encountered were true. They didn't know what to think at that moment. Karen tried to put their minds at ease. Telling them she would never hurt any of them.

As Karen talked to the others she finally convinced them that they were safe with her. After they talked they decided to explore the other room. Entering the other room they discovered it was lit up better so they could see the whole room. The only thing in the room was a round slab made out of metal. On the metal were pictures of four creatures that looked like the statutes once aging. It was clear to Karen that these creatures were of great importance.

Karen and the others had already destroyed a couple of these statutes. She was wondering if these creatures were considered gods or if they were the god's army. She just knew she didn't want to fight them anymore. In the middle of the metal slab where the ancient text that reads " The blood of the beast will free them all.

No one knew what this meant. Was it to free whoever lived there, or to free all creatures that they saw as statutes? Could it mean it would free them of all the evil that is now after them for the treasures they have taken? They wondered if they really wanted to find out.

One of the people that was with Karen swore that if he made it off the island he would never go on any more adventures aging. For he had all he could take and now all he wanted to do was to finish this adventure.

They decided to leave the room without figuring out the text. They didn't want to waste any time. They interred the hallway again, going future down into the ruin. Only to enter a huge room at the end of the hallway. Lit up so bright by the touchers. The light of the fire was reflected off the gold-plated walls.

The room was so bright it hurt everyone's eyes. They held one hand over the top of their eyes to block the light the best they could. As they explored the room. In this room, there was a huge chair made of gold with diamonds and rubies decorated the chair and gold satin cushions laid upon the chair. Purple curtains flowed down from the ceiling all around the room. A red carpet covered the floor. Right in the middle of the room was the biggest chest they had seen so far. A large statue of a Phoenix is set on both sides of the chair.

Around the chest was a ring of fire. It was cold to the touch. Everyone thought it was crazy. The rug had several purple satin cushions spread all over it. Karen and the others examined the room. They scoured the area for whatever they could find.

After looking under every cushion they saw and finding nothing. Karen turned her attached to the chest in the middle of the room. As she reached into the fire it became hot. And the longer Karen kept her hand in the fire it got hotter. She knew they had to find another way to get to the chest.

They looked around even more until Karen saw a hole right in front of the fire. It didn't look like a keyhole so someone mentioned that Karen should try her gold dagger. So Karen plucked her dagger out of her pocket and stuck it into the hole, which did exactly what she needed to do to extinguish the fire.

But when she pulled the dagger out of the fire it lit back up. So stuck the dagger back into the hole, putting out the fire again. This time she left the dagger in so they could reach the chest. To unlock the chest, they had to arrange symbols. A series of four symbols must be arranged in a particular order.

A selection of twenty-five symbols was available to them. They spent around twenty-five minutes figuring out the symbol combination. After getting the combination they hurried up to open up the chest. While opening up the chest they were shocked at what they saw. There was only one item in the chest. It was a small flat crown and on the back of it was a rod. It looked like a key, except that it had a rod that was attached to the flat side of the crown, rather than the point.

Karen kept the crown as a key. Since the chest had nothing else in it, they closed it up and Karen removed the dagger from the hole, causing the fire to reappear. Following Karen's placement of the dagger and key-like item into her bag. As they were leaving the room a flash of light hit Karen and the other. When the light faded away they saw they were outside of the ruin.

Standing back in front of the tree with the door on it. Their escape from the ruin confirmed the presence of magic on the island. Karen was usually really good at finding her directions anywhere she was at. But this time she was confused and could not find her way. No matter what she did the island itself was moving all around. It even seemed nature was playing tricks on them.

So Karen led the group off to the left which seemed to even go deeper in the jungle. They seemed to walk for days. During which they ate berries and twigs wherever they could find them. They would fill up their water containers everywhere they could find sufficient water. During the fifth day of travel, they stumbled across three large and five small ruins.

Karen made the decision to explore the small ruins first. Upon doing so, all they found was an enormous pole in the middle of the room with a huge long chain attached to it. In all five small ruins like they were a big dog house for some huge creature.

So now all that was left was to explore the three big ruins. Karen chose to check out the ruin on the right. Mike touched a strange statue as they approached the ruin. When he touched it Mike yelled out in pain then vanished into thin air. Karen and the other members scream out loud from what they saw.

In an attempt to be safe from what made Mike vanish, they both ran to the ruin as fast as they could in hopes that it would not happen to them. They were terrified that they might die on the island too.

Karen and Mary took caution as they interred the ruin. Upon entering the ruin, they found themselves in a large room filled with what looked like bunk beds. The room looked like it could hold hundreds of people. While searching the room they found a door off on the left side of the room. Going into the door and down a dark damp hallway.

Which seem to be leaning down as if they were going down a ramp. As they reached the end of the hallway. They entered a room and they saw something that looked like a fire pit made of stone. There was a pile of ash at the bottom of the fire pit. On the other side of the fire pit was a staircase that led up. Karen led the way up a flight of stairs into another gigantic room.

In this room were stone slabs set upon other stones making them look like tables. Karen thought it must be some kind of lunchroom because there were so many of them. The stone table and stone benches were the only things in the room.

As they looked around the room they saw another door at the end of the room. Going through the door they walked right into a room. It had two chairs made of metal with animal hides for cushions. A sword was propped up against one of the chairs. With a small crown placed in the chair. In the middle of the chairs was a table made of wood. Placed on it was a metal cup. There looked to be footstools in front of the chairs. Animal hide was laid all over a dirt floor.

The ceiling had a round opening in the middle of it. Right below the opening in the ceiling was a stone table. There were what looked like knives on the table. On each Connor of the table, there is a metal ring. At one end there was a skull-shaped cup on the table. The walls were decorated with skulls. There was a path of bones leading from the chairs to the table in the center of the room. A door on the left of the room was framed with bones, and the corners were adorned with two skulls.

Karen and Mary searched the room to see if they could find anything. Unfortunately, nothing worthwhile could be found in this room. So they decided to leave the room. As they stepped outside the boned framed door, they found themselves outside in front of the third ruin. All three ruins seem to have been linked by the interior hallways.

Considering that it was getting late, Karen decided they should camp at the ruins for the night. Their agreement was to switch off sleeping during the night. Sleep every four hours before switching. In order to maximize their chances of being safe.

During the night Karen was woken by Mary. Since the strange noise was getting closer and closer, she was concerned for their safety. In the event that they had to fight for their lives, they both grabbed their machetes. Suddenly, the jungle was filled with frightening eyes. Despite their efforts to hide, they froze in fear. The eyes were getting closer as they watched.

Getting ready for a battle, Karen steadied herself. Now at this point, the eyes were just on the edge of the jungle. Then suddenly there was a loud roar. An explosion of light flashed down into the third ruin, illuminating the ruin. There were chanting sounds coming from inside. Karen was unable to understand any of the chanting; it seemed to be in a language she had never heard. Karen was terrified, yet also fascinated by it.

Karen was compelled to investigate the strange events. Karen and Mary decided to explore the ruin which was lit up. The eyes from the jungle passed right by them going into the ruin. It was just eyes, nothing else, just hundreds of pairs of eyes. As Karen watched, her curiosity was sparked.

After Karen watched all the eyes pass by. Following them, Karen stopped at the door of the ruin to watch. Her eyes filled with terror as she saw what was going on. All of a sudden the eyes now had human bodies. In the two chairs were two creatures.

With the heads of beasts and the bodies that looked like humans. They had two horns on top of their heads and one in the center of their forehead. Having glowing red eyes and teeth that look like fangs. With dark green tent-like skin.

One of the creatures that had a crown on his head appeared to be the ruler. He pointed to the table and said some strange words. Mary, who was with Karen appeared on the table as soon as he said those words. Despite her desire to scream, Karen was too scared to do so. Her desire to run was conflicted with her desire to help Mary. Despite her fear, she stayed in case she could rescue Mary.

Standing around the table, all the humans started chanting again. As well as doing some kind of dance. As the chanting dance continued, four figures in black robes appeared around the table. Karen was unable to determine if they were humans or something else. The four black figures began chanting in a different language than the others.

The light that came down from the sky grew brighter. The humans stopped chanting and sat down on the animal skins lying on the floor. The black figures started to sway in a forward and backward motion as they began to chant louder. The light from the sky turned red. As the black figures picked up a knife from the table, they stopped chanting.

Karen is fearful of what may happen. Knowing that it was hopeless, she did not attempt to save Mary. Almost instantly, the black figures plunge their knives into Mary. Instantly killing her. Within a moment, every human and beast vanished into thin air. As the light from the sky faded, the ruin began to grow dark again. There was only one body in the ruins: that of Mary who was killed on the table.

When Karen ran for her life, she grabbed her bag along the way. She ran all night without ever looking back. The only time she stopped was when morning came. Resting for a short period of time before continuing. Know now exactly why the locals were terrified of the island. Now Karen was afraid of the dangers on the island.

Karen walked for a couple of days, sleeping only a few hours each night. She ate whatever she could find. As she drank her last drops of water. Throughout the whole time, she had one question on her mind. What were her chances of escaping from the island?

Karen's possessions included gold, rubies, and some very rare artifacts. That she collected on the island. With all these treasures, Karen would be extremely wealthy. Once she got back to Illinois. However, she must first leave the island. It is something she hopes to accomplish very soon.

A few hours into her second day of walking she encountered another ruin. Now Karen must choose between exploring the ruin or continuing to walk. She decided to investigate the ruin after pondering it for some time. The ruin's exterior was mostly covered in vines, twigs, and branches of every kind.

Her attention was drawn to ancient writings above the door as she got close to it. It read "Here lay the great king". At that moment, Karen realized she was staring at a tomb. The fact that it was probably the safest place on the island convinced Karen to go inside. Most cultures would avoid tampering with a tomb due to the fear of a curse that would destroy them.

In order to be able to see inside, Karen broke a stick that was large enough to make a touch. Having set it on fire. Karen walked into the tomb. The interior of the building was dark and cold. Pictures covering the walls seemed to tell the life of the king. Karen found all the wonderful pictures to be very interesting.

Karen walked for about fifty feet down this dark, damp hallway. Walking into the room, she saw more pictures on the wall. In the center of the room was a stone table. There was a chair at the opposite end of the table. In addition, there were two doors.

The pictures Karen looked at told her a story about a king and what she thought was a god. She thought the god she saw was the same as the two figures she saw in the ruins she had run from a couple of days ago. In the pictures, this half-beast, half-human figure appeared taller than the human.

Karen assumed the human in the picture was the king. It appears that the king gave gifts to the god in the picture. Additionally, the images appeared to show the god instructing the king. A guide to how to sacrifice someone to a god. In order to gain certain rewards that he might need for his kingdom.

When Karen has finished viewing all the images, she tries to open one of the doors. Only to her surprise when she discovered it was just a space to hold a big statue. This statue depicts a half-human half-beast figure. Like the images on the walls and like the figure at the ruin. So Karen moved to go through the other door. When she opened it was another hallway that led to two more doors.

Karen opened the door on the left. After opening the doors, she found four stone tables with mummies on top.

Karen knew it was a burial chamber. There are cultures that buried other people with the kings so they could care for the king in the afterlife. Since the mummies and the tables were the only things in the room. Karen went to check out the other room.

Interrent the other room she discovered several pots. Broken pot pieces were also present. The pots were plan and made out of clay. Karen thought this might be when they placed food and drink for the king to have in his afterlife. Karen could not find anything of real value in the room. However, she found another door leading straight into a different room.

This room had several containers filled with gold, rubies, and diamonds. Karen knew this was the treasurer for the king to have in his afterlife. It also had crowns made from gold, along with satin purple satin robes. Some armor made of gold, and some made of plain metal.

Karen's bag was almost full so she could not take much. She took a few handfuls of diamonds and rubies. Placing them in her bag before she left the room. She left through the door opposite the one she entered. Walking down another hallway lined with what looked like armed soldiers. They held golden swords and wore gold armor. Their purpose was to protect the king after his death.

Knowing the king's resting chamber wasn't far. Continuing down the corridor, Karen found herself in a large room. Within the room, there were more images covering the walls. The images seem to describe how the king imagined his afterlife would proceed. How he had immense power he would use to rule over millions of people. How he would be worshipped by his people.

In the center of the room was a huge sarcophagus. Made from gold and adorned with diamonds and rubies. The top had an image of a man wearing gold armor holding a huge gold sword. On top of his head was a gold crown. The sarcophagus was set atop a stone table.

In each corner of the room was another armed soldier. That looked just like the ones in the hallway. Each one was facing the gold sarcophagus. At the end of the room were six huge golden chests filled with gold, diamonds, and rubies. Karen knew she was in the king's burial chamber.

After exploring the tomb Karen was still terrified of what was on the island. It was impossible to tell whether she would sleep safely that night. She had to decide to go back into the jungle or stay in the tomb for the night. She walked back through the tomb to where she interred it. She stayed in the tomb, knowing she was close enough to the outside to escape if necessary.

Despite her efforts, Karen only managed to get a few hours of sleep before aerie noises woke her. She reaches for her machete to protect herself. Not knowing if the noises are coming from inside or outside. She stayed where she was to hopefully be safe. She waited until she knew where the strange sounds were coming from. This would enable her to know where to go for safety.

Despite the danger, she managed to stay safe. In the morning Karen left the tomb. She was hoping she was headed to the seashore. So she could catch the boat and leave the island. There seemed to be a slow thinning out of the jungle. As a result, Karen had an easier time walking through.

Karen came up to a large river. At this point, she was unable to cross the river due to its rapid pace. So she followed the river downstream. She was hoping it would lead her to the ocean. As she followed the river, she started noticing strange-looking animals around her. As Karen grew increasingly worried, she did not know if the animals were going to attack or not. The animals looked as if they came out of some kind of Syfy movie.

The ones that had a little bit of a resemblance to birds. The birds looked like a mixture of a pterodactyl and a bald eagle. Some of the animals were on the ground. Looked like a mixture of a monkey and a bandicoot. Others resemble a mixture of a zebra and a leptocyon. All the animals seem to be a mixture of modern animals and dinosaurs.

The future Karen followed the river the stranger the animals got. Some got bigger while others got smaller. Karen kept a close eye out on everything around her. This island's inhabitants had already attempted to kill her several times.

As the dawn of night was near. Karen saw what looked like a small village. She hopes to find some other people there for her safety. She realized, however, that the village was empty as soon as she got close to it. People could be heard far away, however. Wasn't sure if it was safe to hide or run before they got close.

So that she could tell if she would be safe, Karen decided to get a closer look at the people. As she approached, she kept a safe distance away from them in case she had to run for her life. Watching from among some bushes. That kept her hidden from all the people.

Some people seemed to be gathering some food from a garden. Others were fishing in the river. Some were gathering water in larger pots. All of them looked normal, which made Karen happy. But she decided to watch them a little bit longer. Even though she was extremely hungry and thirsty.

As the people finished gathering food and water. They started walking back toward the village. Karen was still feeling nervous and had no idea what to do. In order to protect herself, she remains hidden. After they all walked by and no one saw her. She waited a little while longer before sneaking down to the garden and river.

To gather herself as much food and water as she could carry. Trying to remain as quiet and concealed as possible. As night fell upon Karen she heard some music. Along with some chanting. Having to examine what was occurring more closely. She snuck up closer to get a better look.

What she saw was a huge fire in the middle of the village. With people dancing and chanting around it. It was the same kind of chanting she heard in the ruin a few days ago. After a little bit, a creature stepped out from one of the huts. It looked like the creature in the ruin and the stature in the tumb.

The people worshiped this creature. It came clear to Karen she was not safe with these people. So she stayed hidden for her safety. As she kept watching what was going on in the village. This creature seemed to be a god to these people. It was twice as big as them. It stood by the fire and pointed over to the left of him to another hut. Out came eight men carrying a woman on a wooden slab. She was dressed up more than the other women in the village.

As they approached the creature. A ball of fire fell from the sky. Landing into the fire then the creature roared out so loud it seemed to echo across the land. When he was done the woman that was carried out was placed on the ground. She stood up and kneeled down to this creature. The rest of the people did the same thing kneeling down to this thing.

Then the creature placed his hand on her head. While doing some kind of wired chant. After he was done four figures in black picked up the woman and threw her into the fire. She never put up a fight to save her own life. After she was thrown into the fire. The fire turned into blood when the creature walked into it. Almost as though he enjoyed getting covered in blood.

As he stood in the blood the people began to chant again. After a few minutes, the blood turned back into the fire. He stayed in the fire for a little bit longer. There was no indication that it hurt him. After about ten minutes the creature walked out of the fire and went back into the hut it came out of. The people kept on chanting and dancing half the night.

When there was no more noise coming from the village. Karen snuck away from there as fast as she could. Down by the garden and crossing the river to the other side. She hopes to get far enough away by morning.

As morning seemed to come early. Karen had to find someplace to hide to get a little bit of sleep. Before she would pass out. Finding an empty cave seemed to be a stroke of luck for her. She covered the entrance up as much as she could. Before she lays down to get some sleep.

After waking from a well-deserved nap, Karen reevaluated her day. She didn't know how much more she could take; she just knew she had to get off the island. So she cleared the cave's entrance. Then grabbed her bag and headed out of the cave. Walking for hours when she found another cave.

After checking it out she planned to spend the night. Branches and leaves were arranged over the entrance as a bit of a safety measure. Not wanting to build a fire for warmth. She covered herself with big leaves to keep warm. As well as to hide her even more from all the weird creatures on the island.

Fortunately, she managed to get a full night's sleep that night. Before leaving the cave she had a little bit to eat and drink. Praying that she would not run into anything else that would hurt her. Or want to kill her. She just wanted off this crazy island. Karen loved adventures but she had never had to fight for her life on any of them before.

After having her breakfast and leaving the cave. Karen noticed as she walked the animals were looking normal now, which gave her a bit of comfort. She was hoping that all the dangers of the island would be gone now too. She also believed she was now closer to the ocean. Where she would catch her boat and go home.

The island does hold some weird and strange things. There was a magical element to it. In addition, there are also some that aren't found anywhere else in the world. The idea that some may have come from another world also occurred to Karen. Taking a deep breath, she knew she never wanted to visit this place again or mention it ever.

But the more she walked the more she started to believe. She was never going to be able to leave this nightmare of an island. She walked all day and rested every few hours. To keep her strength in case she had to fight for her life again.

Once again, nightfall ushered in the need for a safe place to sleep. So far, there was no safe place insight. It seemed as if her thoughts were consumed by concern about her safety throughout the night. The air was filled with more strange sounds. She kept her machete in her hand the entire time. Just in case there is something that might happen, she will be prepared.

About an hour and a half later, she noticed an unusual building. The darkness made it impossible for her to tell whether it was a ruin or a dwelling. Knowing she had to take her chance. Karen entered the old dwelling. Finding a way to light up a touch so she could see. There was also an aerie smell coming from the dwelling. The smell was so bad that it made Karen sick to her stomach.

Inquiring what made that smell, she looked around the house. Also, to find anything that could help her stay safe. The dwelling seemed to be one big room. Within the room was a bed placed up against the wall. Beside the bed was a small table. At the foot of the bed was an old trunk. In the middle of the room was a table with two chairs. Across from the bed was a fireplace. With a stack of firewood beside it. An old metal pot is set in the middle of the fireplace.

Above the fireplace hung two swords. Karen thought they would be useful for the rest of her time on the island. On the table were the words carved on it that read. " To get on was easy. To escape, you must use the dagger that slays the beast. A crown fits no king. To unlock the door you can not see". This confused Karen a great deal. What could it all mean?

As she tried to sleep that night. The words on the table kept going through her head. She tossed and turned all night. She had a restless night due to this. Getting just a little bit of sleep. After waking up, she glanced at the words written on the table and tried to figure out their meanings. There was no way she could forget these words. For they served a purpose that was unique to them.

There was still a foul smell in the dwelling. That appears to have worsened overnight. Karen saw nothing in the room to give off any kind of smell. So she decided to leave the dwelling. When she went outside, she quickly realized what was causing the smell.

On the side of the dwelling, in a nearby tree, was one dead body. They were dressed in modern clothes. Karen Knew right then that John was hung in the tree. It brought her back to thinking about the words on the table. It was easy to get on the island. Were they killed because they lacked the dagger or this crown to open a door they couldn't see?

Karen was afraid to cut him down. For who or whatever put them there might come for her. So she left the dwelling thinking that she had a dagger, could it be the dagger that was needed? But how could a dagger be made of gold? Be the dagger to slay the beast? Could the beast be the thing that the islanders are worshiping?

Karen also remembered that she did have a key-like item that had a crown on it. No king could wear that crown. Could she escape from this horrifying place with the items she had? She was going crazy thinking about it. But yet a couple of questions were on her mind. Did she have to fight this crazy-looking beast? How could she find a door you could not see?

She remembered she helped to kill beast-looking statues but not with any dagger. She walked for another day. Sleeping in a pile of brush to stay safe. On the next day, Karen saw another ruin. It is set just at the edge of the jungle. She could see the ocean right behind it.

Karen tried to go out around the ruin. But every time she tried the ruin would move in the same direction she did. There was no other choice but to investigate this ruin as well. She hated to do it for she knew every time she went into one. There was a great chance she could die. She was terrified that she would have to fight the beast in this one. She wondered if she would still be safe if she had left all that treasure she had taken.

Was it too late now to leave the treasure? Karen decided to keep all that she had taken. For it only matched some of the warnings. But it did not match the words on the table. She was determined to keep it all because of what she went through. Karen took in a few deep breaths and headed for the door on the ruin.

On top of the door in ancient writings were the words " Enterer here die here". It sent chills up Karen's spine. Before she reached the door. It slowly began to open up on its own. After she eased through the door. The door slammed shut behind her. Hearing loud screams coming from further inside the ruin.

In fear of her life, Karen wanted to flee. She grabbed both swords she took from the dwelling a few days ago. Hoping that they would help her kill whatever was in the ruin. She slowly moved down the hallway. That was lit up. The walls were covered by images of beast-like creatures. That looked like the creatures she saw before.

The hallway is divided at the end going to the left and the right. She decided to go to the right. Walking about sixty feet before she saw a door. As she opens the door. Only to see four beds in it, two on each side with a table next to the wall in the middle of the beds. Excited to see nothing else.

Going back down the hallway about twenty more feet. Coming to a door on the left side of the hallway. In this room, there were what seemed to be two bunk beds. One on each side of the room. Up against the wall between the beds was a table and four chairs. Nothing else was in the room. As she went back down the hallway she heard loud screams. But could not determine from which direction they were coming from.

Gripping the swords tighter as she walked down the hallway. Until it opened up into a huge room. In the room were two huge chairs at the end of the room. That looked like they were made from gold. On the top of the chairs were rolls of diamonds. The chairs were up on a platform. From the door to the platform was a red rug.

The walls were also made of gold. With ancient writings on them. Karen could not understand the writings. Also on the walls were images of battles. Between humans and the creatures, she had seen all over the island. In most of the battles, the humans were killed. However, in one set of images, the human killed the creature. Using a gold dagger-like she had.

It showed how the human killed the creature. By stabbing it in the right side of its chest. Karen was aware she must remember this in case the warring was true and she had to fight the creature. Also in the images of the human killing the creature. It showed the human taking blood from the creature. As well as the human going out by the ocean and throwing the blood in the air out toward the ocean. The blood seems to hit an invisible wall. As it hit it seemed to bring up a place to put the crown.

When the crown was placed in it the human was able to go to the ocean and get on a boat. Karen knew now that the only way off the crazy island was to fight the creature's so-called beast for her life and freedom. Karen had a plan now because it was pictured on the wall's now she had to find the creature.

There was nothing else in the room and the only way out was the way she came in. So she turned around and walked back down the hallway. Until she reached the point where it had spit. Then she went straight ahead. She passed six doors that she could not open. When she finally opened one on her left.

In the room lining, the wall were weapons of all kinds. Above the weapons were shields. Karen decided to take a shield with her. Picking up different ones to check the weight and size. So she could pick the one she thought would be the best. To protect her in the fight. Which she knew was coming. She wanted to find everything she could to help her with the fight.

Karen also needed to find something she could put some blood in. So she could throw it at the invisible wall. When she got outside. There was nothing in the room to put blood in. Going back down the hallway. Checking out five more rooms that only had chains hooked to the walls. She thought they were rooms where they kept people.

The next seven rooms she checked out had rolls of beds. That filled the seven rooms. So she kept exploring, still trying to find something to put blood in. When she got to the end of the hallway. She saw only two doors. One small one and one larger one. Going through the small one first. She found several pots and bowls made from stone. Of all different sizes and shapes.

Now she had to go through them to find one that she thought would be a perfect size. Searching the pots and bowls for around thirty minutes until she picked the one she wanted. But she was still not wanting to fight this creature by herself. Wishing the others that came with her had served to help her fight and make it home.

Now it was time to check out the bigger door. She knew she had to find the creature. Since the door was three times bigger than all the other doors. Karen believed this would be the room that held the creature. So she pulled out her dagger, placing her bag on her back. Holding the shield in front of her she interred the big boor.

What she walked into looked like a big arena. The kind in ancient times. As she looked around she saw about Big walls. On top of the walls straight from the door were two large chairs. That looked like they were made out of gold. Purple fabric hung behind the chairs. Also along the side of the chairs. On the wall in front of the chairs hung a banner with ancient writing on it. The kind Karen could not make out.

On both sides of the purple fabric on the walls were benches. The floor was made from dirt. Suddenly noise filled the room. That sounds like people cheering. As Karen looked around People appeared on the benches. Two creatures showed up on the two golden chairs. One of them stood up and made some weird noises. Then pointed to Karen. When the door behind her opened up again. Karen was terrified. She believed it was time to fight for her life and her freedom.

As she watched, a creature walked through the door. It wasn't carrying any kind of weapon. Karen thought it didn't need any. As it moved closer to Karen the people started to cheer again. The creature took a swing at her. In a flash, Karen bent down. She steadies her stance to get ready to make her move. The creature moved in closer and Karen swung her dagger. Just missing the creature by inches.

The creature stepped forward as she stepped back. The creature takes another swing at Karen, docking her on her bum. In gaining her footing, Karen was able to cut the creature's leg. Karen drew blood to the people's cheers. The creature became extremely mad as a result. Swing several times at Karen. This resulted in her arm being cut up. Attempts were made by Karen to move out of the way.

The creature was stabbed on the left side of the chest by Karen as she swung back. As the creature continued to swing, she was able to block a few of them. Karen kicked one of the creature's legs from underneath him. Knocking it on his butt. Karen saw her opportunity to stab the creature on the right side of his chest when it fell to the ground. To finally, kill the creature and obtain the blood she needed. The people cheered with excitement as she stabbed the creature. As she watched the creature die on the ground before her, she realized the fight was over.

She took the bowl out of her pact to collect the blood she needed. As she started to collect the blood Karen realized the people and the creatures. Those watching vanish just as quickly as they appeared. Then she cut open the stomach of the creature. She collected the blood she needed. The creature also disappeared soon after.

As Karen looked around the arena started to disappear right in front of her eyes. As it vanished Karen realized she was outside. The arena was not all that vanished; the whole ruin did as well. Having to find invisible walls were now Karen's job. Karen placed one of her hands out in front of her. Trying to see if she could feel the invisible wall.

Slowly, she walked toward the ocean. She was able to feel the wall after about forty feet. She threw a little bit of blood on it. Unfortunately, it did not indicate where to place the crown key. So she smeared the blood all around. Trying to find the place she needed for the crown-like key. Three-fourths of the blood was gone. Fearing she might never find it, Karen became frantic. Ten minutes went by when Karen finally found the place.

Karen was thrilled that she would be escaping this hellish island. After placing the crown key into its slot. Karen now had access to the ocean as the wall disappeared. When the wall came down and Karen walked up the coast, she was surprised to see a boat appear out of nowhere. Karen was unsure whether taking the boat was a good idea or not. All she knew is she wanted to get off the island.

The chance was too good to pass up for Karen. She loaded all her belongings into the boat. She pushed it into the water a little bit. Until she was waist-deep in water. As she climbed into the boat, she felt some relief. The only thing left to do was to find a ship. Which was to roll ten days to Africa.

In her efforts to escape the island, she started rolling. Trying to roll as far as possible before resting. Karen's thoughts are constantly focused on those who did not make it off the island. There wasn't much she knew about them. Her curiosity led her to wonder if they had any relatives in Africa.

Karen decided when she returned to Africa that she would find out if they had any family. Nevertheless, she had to get through the ocean trip first. It was getting late and soon it would be night. As a result, she decided to rest for the night. Hoping the boat will float toward Africa instead of returning to the island.

She woke up the next morning feeling refreshed. Ready to continue rolling away. In the process of rolling away, Karen experienced hunger pains.

But she only had enough water to last a few more days and nothing to eat. Her only wish is to be found and helped to reach Africa. Unfortunately, that wasn't the case that day. Karen found it increasingly difficult to roll the boat the next morning. Because of an absence of food and a lack of water.

She had to stop rolling after a few hours due to becoming weak. She passed out a short time later. She was awoken later by a horn. Her eyes viewed a ship in the distance. Her goal was to draw attention to herself among the people on the ship. She had to wait about an hour for the ship to get close enough for her to board.

As soon as Karen boarded the ship, she received food and water. After that, she took a shower and changed into fresh clothes. After that, she was taken to her room so that she could rest more. Furthermore, she could store her belongings in a safe place.

However, she spent some time looking through her treasures after she reached her room. Making decisions about what to give to the families of those who came to the island with her. Several pieces of rubies and gold were chosen by her to give to them. Following her choice of what to give. It was important to choose the right spot to hide all of the treasure.

Under the bed, she found a weak spot on the floor. There were a few pieces of metal she could lift up. She was able to hide all of the treasure under that. Trusting that it was all safe. She covered it again with the bed. Then turned in for the night. Knowing the fact that Africa was only a few days away. The experience made Karen feel grateful that she was still alive and safe. As a result, she was able to go home.

It didn't take her long to realize that some of the people on the ship discovered she had some riches. Karen was on high alert for anything potentially dangerous. Making sure that she was prepared at all times. As well as staying in her room as much as possible. Only came out to get something to eat.

It was on the third day aboard the ship that two men broke into Karen's room. They were looking for the treasure that they heard she possessed. Unfortunately, Karen stumbled upon them while they were searching her room. Within seconds of Karen entering the room, they attacked her.

During the struggle, one of the men grabbed her and the other punched her. Then move her away from the door. They demanded that she reveal where the treasure is located. She refused to provide them with the information. Her actions only made them angrier with her. Resulting in them punching her even more. Despite this, she still refused to tell them.

A few minutes later, some people in the hallway heard what was happening. And came into the room to help Karen out. They grabbed the two men and pulled them away from Karen. They were then taken away to be locked up. Then the wounds on Karen's face were bandaged.

Fortunately, Karen had only to make it on the ship for a couple of days more. Until they reached Africa. Karen felt as if the days were dragging by. She couldn't wait to get off the ship. Her thoughts had been focused on it since she was attracted. Karen's next two days were peaceful. There was nothing she cherished more than peace. Finally, she reached Africa. She pulled out all of the treasure she hid. After that, she left the boat.

Now it was time to look for family members of the people who went to the island with her. She went to the bars where she found the people who went with her. Karen talked to several people and found out that the families resided in a few villages away. To get to the first village, Karen got a ride. It was at least an hour away.

When she arrived, she knew the gold and rubies would be helpful. Her first task was to locate the two families that lived there. She found them after a few minutes of searching. That was the hardest part of all, having to explain how their relatives died. Karen then presented them with gold and rubies. She then told them their relatives wanted it this way. To provide them with a good life.

Following that, Karen headed towards the next village. Where three more families lived. Karen provided the same service to the three families in the village, as well. All that was left was the village of the last three people. These families received the same care from Karen that she gave to the other families. Karen spent all of the day visiting the eight families.

However, she wasn't able to board a plane until two days later. Her next step was to find a safe place to stay for a couple of days. Her search led her to a small village where she believed it would be safest. She was able to rent a small hut. Now she had to conceal the remainder of her treasure.

However, there was not much in the hut. There is only a bed, table, and two chairs. There was also a dirt floor in the room. Therefore, there was no place to hide the treasure. 'Karen' dug a hole under the bed in order to conceal the treasure. In order to cover it, she took as much cushion as she could. Create the illusion that she did not dig up the floor.

During the next two days, Karen spent all her time in the hut. Just to make sure she wasn't in harm's way. Karen just keeps thinking about going home. With all the treasure she had. In addition to everything, she could possibly get it. With ways in which she could provide assistance to her family. To purchase a house for herself and maybe her parents as well. Purchase a new car as well. As she thought of all the things she had on her mind, she was overwhelmed. But first, she would have to find a way to convert everything to money.

During those two days, time passed slowly. The day had finally come to catch the plane home. The next step was to retrieve the treasure and head to the airport. After she got there, she discovered she had to catch another plane in New York. Karen thought that New York would be the best place to convert into money.

A few minutes later, Karen was ready to board the plane. She was able to get a first-class ticket. Now that she had overcome the danger, Karen thought it was over. It was safe now for her. Her flight took off about ten in the morning.

In the middle of her flight, the plane developed some problems. In Karen's mind, it was just some turbulence. After the pilot got on the speaker and told everyone to buckle up. There was a failure of one of their engines. It is important that everyone holds one. The kind of luck Karen was experiencing was beyond belief. She wondered how much more she would have to endure.

Her memory then shifted to one of the curses on the island. It was coming true that she would still be killed for taking something that wasn't hers? Hasn't this trip already presented enough danger for her? she thought. As soon as the pilot came on the speaker, he told everyone their last engine failed too. The plane was going down in the ocean. Everyone began screaming, and oxygen masks started falling from the ceiling. Everyone was instructed to put on their flotation devices by the pilot.

Upon impact with the water, the plane split into several pieces. The scene was littered with dead bodies. There were only a few survivors of the crash. In an effort to reach a piece of the plane that was floating, Karen and the rest of the survivors did everything they could. When all the survivors were able to get on a piece of the plane. There were only fifteen people left alive, according to Karen.

Karen was fortunate enough to have her backpack with most of the treasure with her. Her swords and shield, which she had taken from the island, were lost. As of that moment, however, she didn't care. Her only concern was that she survived. While horrified that other people lost their lives in the crash, the plane crashed. The crash destroyed the lives of so many innocent people and their families.

The piece of plane Karen was on. There were two other people on it as well. Among them was a young girl who lost both her parents in the crash. Sadly, the other person sustained critical injuries. It wasn't clear whether that person would survive. The ocean was now the biggest challenge Karen and others faced.

Two days were spent floating on the ocean by Karen. Her attention was captured by a distant plane. She tried to get their attention. As she waved her arms and yelled. The plane flew directly over them. Karen was worried they had not seen her. The chance of them being rescued was lost. After that, Karen and the two passengers floated for another couple of hours.

Karen heard another plane. Luckily, this time a rescue aircraft was there to help. Alone with a few more to help all the other survivors. Above Karen and them, an airplane dropped a basket big enough for a person to sit in. Along with a man on another rope. When the man arrived, it was decided that the women who were injured should go up first.

An additional rope would be lowered after that. In that way, Karen could go up, and the man would hold on to the child and go up. After going up, they were flown to the coast of the states. The moment Karen reached the states, she was overwhelmed. Following a medical check-up at the hospital. Karen was cleared to go home.

Karen had to convert the treasure into money now. Nevertheless, Karen went back to Illinois first. Taking a rental car to get back to her town. At this point, she was tired of traveling by plane. Karen had a fear that something was going to go wrong again. In the event, she took another plane.

Things appeared to be going well as she driving home. Before she began to experience car problems, she made it through Pennsylvania and halfway through Ohio. It sounded like the car was knocking. In addition to getting hot. Karen was going crazy because of all the problems she was having. She wondered if the problems would ever end. She had to park beside the freeway when the car stopped running. The only thing she could do was call the toll truck. It took the toll truck only an hour to get to her. The car service sent Karen another car from close by as soon as she reached the garage.

New York and Illinois are only eight hundred and seventeen miles apart. Once she got to Illinois it took her two hours to get home. Karen was delighted when she arrived at her house. For the first time since beginning her journey, Karen was safe from danger. It was now possible for her to convert her treasure into money.

She was ready for a vacation now that she had everything she wanted.
The End

The cruise

Two months have passed since Karen returned from the Unexplained Island. She decided to go on a cruise. A trip around the world. Karen departed on a cruise from California. She had a fancy room. In addition to a bedroom and living area, there was a bathroom and a small kitchen area. In case she desired to prepare something for herself and enjoy cold drinks and snacks.

Among the cruise ship's amenities were a dancing hall, dining room, and playrooms for kids. For people's enjoyment, there was a swimming pool, gym, and theater. It had everything Karen could think of for a good cruise. She was looking forward to a peaceful trip this time. There was no danger surrounding each Connor. She could just relax and enjoy this trip.

For the next five days, it seemed to be perfect. She was having all kinds of fun. Doing everything she could think of on the cruise. Karen was really happy on this cruise. Until the evening of the fifth day. An unexpected storm appeared from nowhere. Thunder echoed throughout the atmosphere as lightning filled the sky. As the heavy rain fell down, you could not see more than ten feet ahead. Karen thought something was weird about this storm. She had never experienced a storm like this before.

When she looked out in front of the ship. Black swirls appeared above the water. Like something out of a movie. Something like a time portal. There was no way for the ship to turn around. There was not enough time to jump on the lifeboats. In Karen's opinion, the only thing she could do to remain safe was to hide. As she prayed for her life. Karen went into the closet to hide. During the storm, it appeared that the ship was being tossed around. Due to the storm, Karen was getting seasick from the movement of the ship.

As quickly as it appeared, the storm went away. It lasted only a few minutes. Then the ship got quiet. Karen stayed in her closet for a few more hours. Before she decided to investigate. But already noticing the ship had changed. Wood had replaced the walls, floor, and ceiling. As opposed to the steal from which they were made. Karen was extremely concerned about this. As she wondered how much of the ship had changed.

While Karen was leaving her room, it was evident that the ship had changed into the wood. She went up to the ship's deck. She was stunned to see her cruise ship transformed into a pirate ship. Her eyes were drawn to the ropes and chains supporting the sails. Along with the helm, from which the captain steers the ship. Over the sails hung a black flag bearing a skull and bones. Members of the crew became pirates. The Captain was a tall, dark man with a black beard and black hair.

The captain was behind the helm. As he yelled Batten down the hatches. It means putting things away and getting ready. During the crew's work, they performed a chantey. This means that they sang a song. Some of the crew was mopping the deck. One of the men climbed a rope going to the crow's nest. Which means the lookout platform. In order to keep an eye out for any other vessels (ships) nearby. Karen stood there in shock. Not knowing what to do. When another pirate touched her on the shoulder. Telling her " have ho" means putting your muscle into it. Then handed her a mop. As a precaution, Karen decided that she should follow what's going on.

While she was mopping the deck. She heard someone yell "sail, ho" which means another ship is in view. Then the captain began to chase the other ship. Then he yelled " All hands on hoy" which means everyone on the deck. As he was telling them to get ready for battle. Upon approaching the other ship, the captain shouted " fire in the hole " as well as " dead men tell no tales ", which is code for an order before a cannon is fired and no survivors. Karen ran to the side of the ship to see what was going on.

When the cannons were shot toward the other ship. Hitting the ship four times. The ship that Karen was on moved right beside the other ship. When the captain yelled "grab your cutlass", he meant a short sword.

Karen grabbed a sword that was beside the berth (the captain's quarters). The other crew members swung over to the other ship using a rope. Started fighting the other ship's crew and captain. Karen was fighting with some of the crew of the other ship after they swung over to the ship she was on.

Karen saw the other ship was sinking when they fought for a short period of time. The captain told everyone to look for the booty (treasure). The crew found eight treasure chests and brought them to the ship Karen was on. Afterward, the captain surveyed the treasures and the prisoners. Karen discovered the name of the ship she was traveling on. It was called the Black Rose which means death.

After all the booty was put up the captain had all of the prisoners line up. Having them walk the plank. One at a time they walked to their deaths. After they all walked the plank. The ship's deck had to be cleaned again by Karen and the crew. As she watched all the men who walked the deck trying to stay alive. By being able to cling to pieces of the other ship. Karen could not believe they were just going to leave these men behind to die. As they sailed away.

The next few days it was just working on the ship. Karen was wondering if she was ever going to go back home. Or would she be stuck in this new time she was in? When she saw something big swimming toward the ship. As soon as the captain heard, he yelled all hands hoy! Karen didn't know what was swimming toward them. She just knew it was really big. Her first thought was that it could be a whale. Until it popped its head out of the water. It looked like something out of the dinosaur ages. It had a big head and a long neck. But it also had tentacles like a squid.

The cannons were loaded by some of the crew, but Karen grabbed her sword to use against the creature. Several tentacles begin to extend from the creature on the ship. As if it were attacking the ship. The cannons were fired at the creature. In addition to the crew cutting and slashing away at the tentacles. In the midst of the fight, Karen saw some of the crew members be tossed into the ocean. Now, the tentacles of the creature appeared on both sides of the ship. As more cannons were fired off. The sails of the ship were damaged. Karen and some of the other crew members were able to cut off a couple of the tentacles. The creature slowly detached its tentacles from the ship and disappeared into the sea after the cannons went off a couple more times.

The captain told the crew to keep whatever part of the tentacles were on the ship. In the event that it was needed, it could become food. Karen did not like that idea. Despite her dislike of seafood, she tried to eat it occasionally. For the sake of survival. Trying to figure out how to get home was now Karen's focus. It was not the cruise she had envisioned for herself. Her trip was meant to be relaxing and luxurious.

It seemed impossible that something so strange and unusual could happen. She prayed that the storm would reappear so that she could return to her former life. In order to leave ocean creatures and pirate ships behind.

Following the fixing of the crow's nest. The person on it yelled, "sail, ho". Karen knew right then another battle was coming soon. The huge ship was sighted to the left of her. Flying a British flag. The captain yelled fire the cannons. The cannonballs hit the ship six times. Black Rose was hit three times by the British ship. On the upper deck. Five times, the black rose fired back at the British ship. As the Black Rose and the British ship approached one another, cannons were fired back and forth until the crew was able to board. Crossing on planks affixed to the ships and swinging across ropes. The Black Rose crew attacked the crew of the British ship.

On both ships, the fight broke out. Clashing of the swords could be heard miles away. In addition to the screams of the crew members from both ships. The fight lasted for a couple of hours. When the crew of the Black Rose beat the British ship. Taking the captain and twenty crew members as prisoners. Along with seven chests full of treasure and all the weapons they could find. They also took all the silver they could find.

After this, the captain ordered the fire to be lit on the ship. However, the Black Rose sailing away from the British ship before it was set on fire.

In response to the captain's order, the booty was put up in his room. After that, he ordered everyone but the captain to walk the plank. It was ordered that the captain be chained below the deck. It would be easy to get a ransom for the British captain if he was returned. But before they could try to get Ransome for the British captain. All the Black Rose's treasure had to be hidden so the British would not get it if anything went wrong.

Therefore, they sailed to a land called the land of no name. Karen was one of the crew members who went to the island to help bury the treasure as soon as they arrived. All the treasure was transported to the island in four rowboats. Karen and the crew member walked for two days before finding the spot where the captain liked to bury the treasure. It took five of the crew to dig the hole and put all the treasure in that hole. Once the treasure had been buried, they headed for the ship.

A half a day away from the ship. They were attacked by a massive creature. That looked like it was a mix of a dinosaur and a monster off of a movie. It looked like a hybrid of a Tyrannosaurus rex and a Kaiju. It was really ugly and strange. However, what wasn't in this wired time zone. Karen and the rest of the crew drew their swords. It's just a matter of time. When the creature swung its arm and hit a couple of the crew members. Cutting them across their chest.

Karen stabbed the creature in his stomach, drawing blood. His arms swung around to try and hit crew members as he roared loudly. Missed Karen's head by inches. When Karen and two of her crewmates stabbed the creature in the chest. As the creature fell to the ground. The Captain chopped off the head of the creature. Karen felt relief knowing the creature was dead.

As soon as the creature was killed, they went to the Black Rose. Therefore, they were able to sail off to the British Isles. To get the ransom for the British ship's captain. To reach the British Isles, they had to travel for five days. Once they arrived there, the captain sent word to the king. Tell him he has the captain, and he wants six hundred and seventy pounds for his safe return. Otherwise, the captain would be killed.

The king sent word back telling the captain. In response, he threatened the crew and the captain with treason charges. The captain then ordered Karen and the rest of the crew. To attack the town and kill as many as they can. While they take whatever treasure they can find. In addition, he had the captain hung. In the middle of the town at night. When they attacked the town.

In order not to hurt anyone, Karen hid. She was not a killer. She waited until sunrise to head back to the ship. So she would not be captured and charged with treason. Then be put to death. Once she got on the ship she hid below the deck. As the ship sailed away from the British isle. Hopefully, the Black Rose will be far enough away that they are safe. So it would be impossible to reach by the British army.

The Black Rose sailed for seven days. Karen was glad the last few days were peaceful. She prayed it would stay this way. In addition to praying that she will be able to return home. Wondering why her last two journeys ended up like a nightmare. She may have been in some weird dream that she can't seem to shake. In any case, all she wanted to do was return to her home.

When all of a sudden Karen was knocked on her butt. By an elongated tentacle of a giant squid. That attacked the ship. The crew was caught off guard. Now they had to fight for their lives once again. The squid's tentacles were coming from both sides of the ship. It was like a panic on the ship with the crew members running everywhere. The fighting and protection of their lives is their number one priority.

During one of the tentacle attacks, Karen was knocked unconscious. The squid pulled its tentacle into the water. Just to wrap it around the ship again. For several minutes, Karen remained unconscious. She was woken up suddenly by water hitting her in the face. Coming off the tentacle of the squid. When it wrapped around the ship. Currently, the ship has six tentacles wrapping around it.

Karen and the crew stabbed and slashed at the tentacles. As they fought the squid. Apparently, the squid was trying to take the ship down into the water. The crew and Karen were able to cut some of the tentacles off. In response, the squid seemed to become quite angry. It rammed the remainder of its tentacles onto the ship. A few crew members were knocked into the ocean.

Swimming for their lives as they tried to avoid the squid. When finally a few of the crew members were able to fire off some of the cannons at the squid. Which put a hole right in the middle of the squid. The squid tentacles slid off the ship into the ocean. When the crew was sure the squid was gone. They hurled ropes down towards the crew in the ocean. So they can pull all of the crew members back on board. There were five crew members killed when they were attacked by the squid.

Karen and several of the other crew members were wounded during the fight. Karen was hating the ocean more and more. She was wondering what more she was going to have to suffer through. Defending the ship from creatures and other pirates. Keep herself alive and safe by doing everything she can. As night fell over the ship. Karen would sleep below the deck. For fear of another attack. She did this for the next couple of weeks.

There was a shortage of food and water on board, so the crew became restless and angry. They started talking about a mutiny. Which means to go against the captain. The captain assured the crew that everything would be fine. There will be plenty of food and water soon for them. Because they were about to land in just a few days. Where they can get all the supplies they need.

When the crew landed, the captain promised they would have a good time for a week. But just after a couple of days the captain ordered the crew back to the ship. For British ship was not too far away. And the captain feared for all their lives. But the crew was mad and wanted what the captain promised them. For they were tired of working and fighting all the time.

The Black Rose was able to escape the British ships once again. The crew started talking about a mutiny again. Karen was mentioned as the person who should replace the captain by some of the crew members. The combination of excitement and fear caught Karen off guard. Knowing if she became captain, her responsibility would be to ensure the crew's safety. Also to collect treasure and share it with the crew.

However, they would need to defeat the captain first. Waiting for the right moment, rising up against him. Two days later, the crew decided to replace the captain. As he ordered the crew to mop the deck. A couple of the crew members grabbed the captain from behind. Telling him his time is up and he will no longer be captain of the Black Rose. Karen was told she was the new captain at that point.

It was her first duty to decide what to do with the old captain. Some of the crew members wanted him to walk the plank. Others were just looking to kill him and throw him overboard. First Karen has to calm the crew down. So she could decide what to do. She chose to force the old captain to walk the plank. Karen figured if he walked the plank. Her actions would not have killed him; they would have given him a chance of survival if found. She knew that was the only way she could keep the crew happy. And it is important for her not to become a killer.

After the old captain walked the plank. Karen had to find a way to make the crew happy. But before she could decide what to do. One of the crew members in the crow's nest. Yelled "Sail, ho!" as Karen looked around she saw a ship behind the Black Rose. Karen yelled, "batten down the hatches" to the crew. She yelled to the one behind the helm to bring a spring upon'er. Meaning to turn the ship around. That way the Black Rose could face the ship that was behind them. In case they wanted to attack the Black Rose.

The other ship fired its cannons at the Black Rose. Karen ordered her crew to fire their cannons back. As the ships got closer to each other.

Karen had all the crew arm themselves with swords to prepare for the battle awaiting them on the ship. Though Karen didn't want to fight, she knew that she couldn't afford it. In order to save as many lives as possible, she had to take her crew into battle.

The cannon smoke filled the air between the two ships. The sound of cannon fire echoed throughout the ships. As the two ships moved beside each other. Planks of wood were placed between the ships. The crew of both ships ran onto each ship. We're now in the midst of the fight. The sound of the swords clashing could be heard for miles. Increasingly loud battle cries emanated from the crews.

Karen was in a fight with the captain of the other ship for her life. The other captain suddenly knocked Karen's sword out of her hand. Then knocked Karen on her butt. While Karen looked up, the other captain's sword came tumbling down towards her. While the sword struck the deck, Karen rolled left. Allowing her enough time to grab her sword and stand up.

Karen swung her sword and sliced off the other captain's head. The body and the head fell to the deck. Immediately after the crew saw that their captain had died, they stopped fighting. They threw down their swords. Told Karen where the treasure was. In response, Karen ordered her crew members to gather all treasures and valuables they could find.

The crew gathered up eight chests full of gold and diamonds. Along with two chests full of rubies. Furthermore, they gathered a number of silver pieces. Karen ordered that all the valuables be stored in her room. When Karen looked at all the prisoners, she gave them the option to either follow her or walk the plank. The Prisoners took an oath to follow Karen.

Karen's crew expanded by thirty new members. Karen ordered the other ship to be durned. After that the following days, everything went smoothly. Karen was able to keep enough food and water. Along with giving them a few fun nights on land. Karen was loved by the crew of the Black Rose as their captain. But Karen knew the peace and quiet would not last long. In order to prepare for her next encounter with another ship or an unknown creature at sea, she tried to get mentally prepared. Since she knew that death was possible at any moment.

But the peace and quiet didn't last long enough for Karen. As she was looking over the side of the ship she heard some singing come from someplace she could not see. The crew members alerted Karen that sirens were causing the singing. Which were evil sea creatures that looked like mermaids. They would sing and lure men to their deaths. Karen knew all the men on her ship were in danger. That is when Karen ordered all the men to be locked below the deck for their own safety. There would be no way to escape the sirens unless all the women on board the ship helped.

As the sirens sang their songs it made the men on the ship. Go crazy trying to get to the sirens. Their songs seem to put the men in some kind of trance. Karen was warned that they might need to fight the men to protect the ship and themselves. Because Karen didn't know where the sirens were, she wasn't sure which way to sail. The men on the ship started fighting trying to get out of the hole. This is what they called the area below the deck.

The men were also yelling to the sirens to come to them. Karen ordered half of the women to barricade the door. To keep the men below the deck and keep them safe. As the women barricaded the door. The music of the sirens was getting louder. Making the men crazier by breaking through the door. Several men began jumping from the ship. So they could get to the sirens. The women started knocking the men out so they could save them from the sirens. There were fifteen men who jumped from the ship and swam out of sight. As the men were out of sight. Karen and the rest of the crew could hear the men scream.

All the men left on the ship were being knocked out. Ten more men leaped overboard. Karen could see the bodies of the dead men floating by the ship. There was nothing she could do to stop the men from being killed by the sirens. Several hours passed by as Karen heard sirens and watched the bodies of crew members float in the water. She felt bad for the men who lost their lives.

Paying that everyone else would be fine. But Karen knew the dangers were not over yet. Karen started seeing several abandoned ships. She believed that the crew of the abandoned ship died at the hands of the sirens. Karen counted around twenty-five abandoned ships.

The fear of the unknown paralyzed Karen. She started to think back to when she was on the unexplained island. The cruise left her wondering if the curse has followed her from the island. Also, she wondered if she could escape from the curse?

It has been a day since they had to contend with the sirens and the abandoned ships. When Karen spotted a couple of ships in front of them. She had to decide to fight them or leave them alone. As she was making up her mind. Another crew member spotted the ships. He yelled to get ready for a fight. Karen knew right then she had no choice but to fight now. They were ordered to pursue the two ships and catch up with them.

When the black rose was close enough Karen ordered the cannon to be shot at both ships. Karen had the black rose goes between the two ships. The crew of the ship could therefore take on both ships simultaneously. Multiple times, she fired cannons at both ships. As the black rose was right in the middle of the two ships. They fired cannons back at the black rose. Hitting the ship multiples times caused damage to the ship.

It broke the mass and the sails came crashing down. Along with four holes on the side of the deck. Additionally, the black rose damaged the other ships. There were holes in their ships. One of them lost its mass and sails. As well as its helm. There were also two large holes in the side of the ship. On the other ship, there were four holes in the side of it. There were two holes that were low enough for water to get into. The ship started sinking as a result of this.

The crew was ordered to swing over and gather all the treasure they could find. Take as many prisoners as possible. A crew from the black rose was fighting with a crew from two other ships. Miles away, you could hear the clash of steel swords with battle cries. Karen was engaged in a fight with both captains. Defending herself against every blow from their swords. One of the captains was killed when Karen managed to stab him in the chest.

Karen was cut across the left arm by the other captain. As a result, she became angrier than before. As she swung her sword, she hit the captain square in the face. Making him back up just a bit to regain his balance. Before he swung his sword at Karen. Telling her, "you're going to die". The response was, "not today," said Karen. The other captain's chest was slashed wide open as Karen hit him. The sword fell to the ground as he grasped his chest. Before he fell to the floor of the beck. Moments before he died.

The crew witnessed the death of their captain. As a result, they stopped fighting. The battle was won by Karen and her crew. All the treasure from the two ships was collected. Prisoners were lined up and counted. Afterward, she had her crew counted in order to determine how many had died. In the fight, sixteen members of her crew were killed. Thirty-five pirates were captured by Karen. All of them had the option of following her or walking the plank. Choosing to follow Karen, they all took the oath. To die even if need be to protect Karen as their new captain.

After all the prisoners took the oat to follow Karen. She ordered the only ship stand beside the black rose to be burned. The other ship sunk into the ocean. As a result of the holes the cannon made. After the ship was set on fire. Karen ordered the crew to fix the mass. This would allow them to sail away. Right after they fixed the mass.

And Karen was ready to sail away. Several strange sea creatures tried to attack the black rose once again. The creatures looked like half-humans and half-mermaids. From all directions, they clambered onto the back rose. Taking the crew by surprise. As they scramble to find their swords. To fight off these bizarre-looking sea creatures. They carried what looked like some kind of wired weapons. They used the weapons like a sword. They used this weapon to attack Karen and her crew.

Two of the creatures attacked Karen. One of them cut Karen on the right leg. As Karen blocked a swing of the other sea creature. When Karen swung her sword, it broke the two weapons the sea creature was carrying. It didn't take long for all the sea creatures' weapons to be destroyed. Several of the sea creatures were killed by Karen and her crew. Some of the creatures then jumped back into the water. The crew and Karen have lost sight of them. When the black rose began to sail away.

The following days were peaceful for Karen and her crew. During which they were able to recover from the battles they had. So she could hide most of the treasure, Karen sailed to the same island the old captain sailed to. Only keeping two chests on the ship. Therefore, they would have enough money to buy what they need. When there weren't any ships to rob.

Karen was also able to give her crew a week on land to have some fun. As well as recruiting a few new crew members. So they could maintain the ship with enough crew members. After a few weeks of peace. An attack was launched from the land. A cannonball hits the black rose. Punch a hole through the top of the ship.

She orders the crew to shoot cannonballs back at the people on land. People on land jumped on boats. Sailing out to the black rose. Karen ordered more cannon fire at the boats and the people on land. A group of people climbed onto the black rose from the boats. Suddenly, a fight erupted on the black rose. During the battle, the clash of swords and battle cry were drowned out by the cannon fire.

The black rose was hit by cannon fire a couple of more times. Making two more holes in the black rose. The holes in the black rose were high enough so that no water could enter. As the crew fought on the deck. Karen had to kill four people from the land. Before they all jumped off the ship and headed back to land. The battle on the black rose was short. Karen and her crew destroyed the village of the people who were attacking them from the land.

Karen ordered the crew of the black rose to sail to an island so that they could repair the damage to the ship. It took two days to get to the island. The ship was repaired to the extent that it was safe to do so. It took a week to make all the necessary repairs. The crew of the black rose spent the week working on the ship and having fun on the island.

After the black rose was all repaired. The crew was ordered back to the ship by Karen. So they could head out to sea again. As far as Karen was concerned, being on the ocean was the only way to get home. Trying to find the storm that had brought her here was the only way she could find a way home. After spending a week at sea, the black rose was attacked once again. A giant creature resembling a squid attacked the ship once more.

The tentacles of the creature reached out to surround the ship. As Karen and her crew, we fighting the giant quid-like creature. The half-human, half-mermaid sea creatures also attacked the ship. Karen was fighting four of the half-human and half-mermaid creatures. Two creatures were killed when she swung her sword. She dodged one of the squid's tentacles. The other creature swung their wired weapons at Karen. She took a blow to the chest. Cutting open her chest a little. She swung her sword again and killed the other two creatures she was fighting.

Karen now focused all her attention on the giant squid. When she cut one of the tentacles, the squid pulled it back into the water. When she looked around, she saw that five of the tentacles had been cut off. Meanwhile, the squid pulled the remainder of its tentacles into the water. Blood covered the deck of the black rose. In the aftermath of the fight, Karen ordered her crew to rest. In order to build up their strength. The next day Karen ordered her crew to clean all the blood of the deck of the black rose. After that, it became peaceful for Karen and her crew again.

When on the horizon, she saw an extremely violent storm. But she was also praying that it could be the kind of storm that could take her home. As Karen kept an eye on the storm she had the crew get ready for the storm. Karen was hoping to see the swirling black hole appear before the ship.

As the storm drew closer the thunder and lighting began. From the look of the storm, Karen assumed it was the same kind of storm that brought her to this ancient time. Where the seas were ruled by pirate ships and sea creatures. Never knew the dangers that were on the horizon. As the Black Rose reached the edge of the storm. When the black swirl appeared in front of the ship, Karen saw what she had been looking for. The crew took cover wherever they could. As Karen braced herself for when the ship entered the storm. Seconds later the ship entered the black swirling hole.

After entering the black hole, the ship became quiet once again. Karen noticed after the ship passed through the black hole. The ship changed again. The wood of the ship changed back into metal. Karen realized she was back in her own time. And the ship was back to a normal cruise ship. Now she just was hoping the rest of the time she was on the cruise was normal. So she could make it home safe.

But as Karen went through her belongings she found several pieces of gold, diamonds, and a few rubies. When she found the treasures in her belongings, she was delighted. To have some of the ancient pieces. That would bring her a lot of money. But knowing no one would believe her when she would tell them the story. Of how she got all the treasure she had. But at the moment she didn't care. Karen was just glad she made it home safe.

Karen just thought that she should be careful about what she wishes for. Because the excitement you get might not be the one you want.

The End

Thanks for reading my book

A little bit about Katharine Niffen. She is an aspiring author, she has a great deal of passion for writing. She enjoys making people smile with her writing. Besides being a loving grandma, she's a caring daughter, and mother. Dedicated to pursuing her dreams.